GERTRUDE CHANDLER WARNER

Mystery
Behind
the Wall

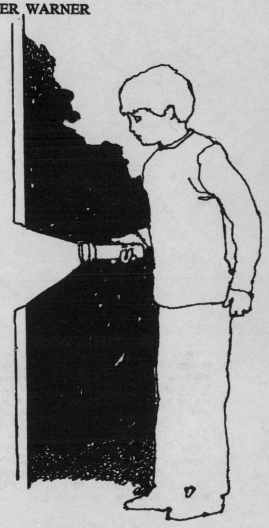

Illustrated by
DAVID CUNNINGHAM

ALBERT WHITMAN & COMPANY· Niles, Illinois

ISBN 0-8075-5367-0

31 32

Printed in the U.S.A.

The Alden Family Mysteries
by Gertrude Chandler Warner

THE BOXCAR CHILDREN
SURPRISE ISLAND
THE YELLOW HOUSE MYSTERY
MYSTERY RANCH
MIKE'S MYSTERY
BLUE BAY MYSTERY
THE WOODSHED MYSTERY
THE LIGHTHOUSE MYSTERY
MOUNTAIN TOP MYSTERY
SCHOOLHOUSE MYSTERY
CABOOSE MYSTERY
HOUSEBOAT MYSTERY
SNOWBOUND MYSTERY
TREE HOUSE MYSTERY
BICYCLE MYSTERY
MYSTERY IN THE SAND
MYSTERY BEHIND THE WALL
BUS STATION MYSTERY
BENNY UNCOVERS A MYSTERY

Contents

Mystery Behind the Wall

CHAPTER 1

Benny's Problem

I don't know what to do with myself," exclaimed Benny one day.

"That's the first time I've ever heard you say that, Benny Alden!" said his older brother, Henry. "What's the matter with you?"

"I tell you I don't know," repeated Benny. "I've got a whole summer vacation and I don't know what to do with it. I've used up one week already. I don't like just to sit around."

He slid down in his chair.

Jessie, Benny's sister, nodded. She said, "You are right, Benny. You worked hard at school all year. And you don't know what to do with a vacation because your friends have gone away. You're lonesome."

"Well, maybe," Benny said doubtfully.

Grandfather Alden said nothing. He liked to let his four grandchildren settle their own problems. He was always there if they needed help. But even Mr. Alden was surprised to hear Mrs. McGregor, the family's housekeeper, put in a word.

Mrs. McGregor had worked for Grandfather Alden for many years. She was there long before the four Alden children came to live with their grand-father. She was a short little woman with grayish-brown hair done in a knot on the back of her head. She never paid any attention to style. She just did the cooking and looked out for the four children and their grandfather.

Now she said to Grandfather Alden, "I know what is the matter. Benny is lonesome, even with a brother and two sisters and a grandfather and a dog and a cat. What he wants is something new and exciting. And I have thought of something."

Grandfather Alden smiled and said, "Let's hear it, Mrs. McGregor. Anything you have to say will interest me, whatever it is."

"Well, as you know, I have a sister living in Canada. She is always writing to me about a neighbor boy who is lonesome, too. He is ten years old now, and an only child. Very few people come out to his place. He seems to be lively, always thinking up something new to do. He works hard, too, to help his father. If he came here for a visit, he'd think this house was wonderful. You wouldn't have to take him anywhere outside these four walls. He'd find plenty to do all by himself."

Benny gave a little jump on one foot. He had a big smile.

"Look at that!" Jessie Alden said. "Benny isn't

lonesome anymore." She smiled at Benny. "You have saved the day, Mrs. McGregor."

"What's the boy's name?" asked Violet.

"His name is Roderick, but no one uses it. Everybody calls him Rory," Mrs. McGregor answered. "If you called out 'Roderick,' he wouldn't even turn his head. His last name is Beaton."

"That's a good name—Rory," said Benny. "I like Rory better than Roderick myself."

The Alden family acted as if Rory Beaton was coming that very day. And he hadn't even been invited!

Jessie said thoughtfully, "Where would you put him, Mrs. McGregor? That empty room next to Benny's is not really a boy's room. The wallpaper has roses, and the pictures are old-fashioned."

"I'll take care of that," replied Mrs. McGregor. "There's a red bedspread I can put in there. Maybe he won't even look at the pictures. He's a busy boy who is forever moving around, doing something. He may tire Benny out."

"A ten-year-old boy tire me out?" demanded Benny. "I'd like to see him do that!"

Then Grandfather put in a word. "You have to fix up his room, Mrs. McGregor, but Benny and the others can help you."

"Let's go," Benny said.

"We'd love to do it," Violet said. "It's fun to fix up a room for company. Let's go now. It will make the time go faster."

Mr. Alden said, "Wait. Might as well finish this business at once. Maybe Rory's parents won't let him come."

"I think his mother will be glad to let him come. She knows I'll be right at hand to take care of him," replied Mrs. McGregor.

The four Aldens smiled to see their grandfather go at once to the telephone. He always did things at once, or not at all.

Mrs. McGregor gave Grandfather the telephone number. Soon he said, "How do you do. Is this Mrs. Beaton?"

Benny could not hear Mrs. Beaton's reply, but he knew his grandfather was pleased. That must mean Rory could come.

Mr. Alden said, "Just as soon as you receive his airplane fare, send Rory along. We will meet him at the airport. Yes, Mrs. McGregor is fine. In fact, she was the one who thought of this plan."

When Mr. Alden put the phone down, he said, "You must remember that the boy comes from Canada and he will not talk exactly the way we do. You will have to be careful about that."

"Oh, we will be," said Violet, "no matter how he talks."

"How soon do you think he'll get here?" Benny asked.

"Three or four days, perhaps," his grandfather answered. "The Beatons will let us know when to expect him."

"Let's get things ready right now," Benny said.

So everyone, even Henry, ran upstairs to fix a room for their Canadian visitor.

"If Rory has the room next to mine," Benny said, "we can rap on the wall for signals." He was making big plans already for his guest.

They opened the door and looked in. "Not much of a room for a boy," said Jessie.

"Not much of a guest room, either," added Violet. "Look at the old-fashioned wallpaper with roses all over it." She pulled up the shades at the windows and the sun shone in.

"That wallpaper has been here for ages," Jessie said. "It was here when we came to live with Grandfather, and it was old then."

Henry said, "I haven't looked around in here for a long time. I think that this was a once girl's room."

Violet nodded. "I have a funny feeling about this room. It seems so sad to me. I don't know why. I guess perhaps it's because it is usually shut up."

Benny was looking at a picture hanging on the wall near the bed. He said, "Look at this old photograph! It's a girl and her family on the front walk of a house."

"Let me look," Henry said. "Why, Benny! It's *this* house—look, you can see the front door and the steps."

"Yes, but—" Benny said. "Our house is much bigger and it has another part over at the side. And the trees and bushes are bigger."

"That picture was taken years ago," Henry said.

Jessie said, "Let's ask Grandfather about it. Maybe the house was changed after this picture was taken."

Violet looked at the picture and the girl. Then she stared at one of the windows in the picture. She saw something no one else had noticed. There was a poster in the window.

"Look!" she said. "There's a poster that says 'Coolidge for President.' Now when was that?"

Henry said, "Well, President Coolidge was elected, let me think, before 1929."

"So that little girl must be pretty old now," Benny said. "I wonder what became of her."

Just then Mrs. McGregor came in with the red bedspread and everyone forgot about the photograph.

Mrs. McGregor said, "Here. Rory will like this, I think."

Jessie said, "That's right. It will make this look more like a boy's room. But Mrs. McGregor, do you remember when Grandfather bought this house?"

"Well, he had it for a short time before I came to work here. I was just a girl myself. I can hardly believe it, but it must have been forty years ago."

Mrs. McGregor shook her head and added, "Time goes by fast when you're busy."

"And slowly when you're waiting for someone," Benny said.

Everyone laughed. Benny and Grandfather were alike—neither of them liked to wait.

CHAPTER 2

A Hole in the Wall

The four Aldens went to the airport to meet Rory. Their grandfather and Mrs. McGregor went along, too. Everyone was excited, wondering what Rory would be like.

"There he is!" exclaimed Benny, waving. "He sees us!"

"My, he's bigger than I thought he would be," Mrs. McGregor said.

Rory proved to be sturdy boy of about ten and also a great talker.

Henry drove, and Rory sat beside him. Rory said, "You're a good driver, Henry. I'm too young to drive a car, but I drive the tractor on our farm."

Benny leaned over the front seat. He said, "How can you drive if you are only ten?"

"It's only at home I drive. Just in the fields. I can't drive a car. I can drive and pull the power-disc harrow and the seeder. But I can't drive a plain car."

Benny laughed. He said, "I should think a plain car would be easy for you."

"Likely it would," agreed Rory. "But I could not run it on the highway. I don't know how to drive in traffic."

The Aldens did not ask about Rory's Canadian speech. It was the other way around. Almost the first thing Rory said was, "Benny, you talk funny. You say 'about the house,' and I say 'aboot the hoose.' "

The Aldens laughed. It was true they and Rory said some words differently. But that just made it more interesting to have a Canadian friend.

"What else do you do on the farm?" asked Benny.

"I help Dad when he has to cut down a tree. After the tree has fallen, I chop off small branches. Then I work with Dad to get the stump out."

"Why?" Benny asked.

"Well, we cut the tree down to make our garden bigger. The stump is in the way. We have a flower garden and a grand vegetable garden, too."

Henry said, "That sounds like hard work."

"Aye, it is," replied Rory. "I mean yes," he added. "My dad is Scottish, you know."

"Like Mrs. McGregor," said Jessie. "She used to call Violet a wee bit of a girl."

"Here we are!" Benny said. "This is where we live, Rory. Everybody out!"

Grandfather said, "Have a good time, Rory. I'll see you at dinner."

Henry and Benny carried Rory's things upstairs.

Benny said, "Want me to help you hang up your clothes?"

"Aye, that I do," replied Rory. He sat down in a big rocking chair and began to rock. He looked around his new room.

"Nice wallpaper," he said. "I like roses. And I like that red bedspread. That is a jolly big closet for one boy. And what's the picture of the house and that pretty little girl?"

Benny laughed. "Rory, you're interested in everything, aren't you? Probably Grandfather can tell you the answers. I don't know."

"Really, I am interested in almost everything," Rory said thoughtfully. He didn't mind having Benny laugh. "I like to know about things," he added.

"Yes, that's what Mrs. McGregor said," Benny replied. Benny took one of Rory's jackets and hung it in the closet. He took a coat and put it in the closet, too.

"That closet looks funny to me," Rory said. "I don't understand it."

"What's wrong with it?" asked Henry, who was going down the hall.

"Well," Rory said, "I thought that closet would be long and go way back. But it doesn't. It's almost square inside."

Benny knocked on the back wall of the closet. It was a wooden wall, not a plastered one.

"I can tell you about that myself," Benny said. "You see my room is next door. My closet backs up to yours. This wooden wall divides the space. Here, I'll draw you a little map."

"I see," said Rory. "The R is for my room and the B is for your room."

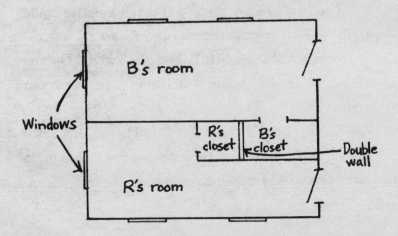

Benny said, "Come in my room and I'll show you."

The two boys ran into Benny's room. Benny opened the closet door and pushed his clothes out of the way.

"See? It's the same wall," Benny said. He knocked on it.

Rory said, "Let me run back to my room. I'll knock on my side."

"OK," Benny said. Soon he heard Rory knocking. But it wasn't as loud as he had thought it would be. He knocked, and in a minute Rory was back.

"Benny, did you hear me?" he asked. "I could hear you knock, but it wasn't very loud."

"Too bad," Benny said. "I was thinking we could signal to each other in the morning."

Rory looked thoughtful. Then he asked, "Do you think we could make a telegraph between our rooms?"

"A telegraph?" Benny asked, and began to see that having Rory around was going to be fun. "You mean run heavy cord from one room to the other?"

"Well, the back walls of the closets are just wood. Maybe there's a crack or a hole we could run a cord through," Rory said.

"And we could hang something heavy that would knock against the wall," Benny said. "Or even a bell."

"That's it," Rory said. "If I pull the rope on my side, it would make a noise on your side."

Benny got his flashlight and the two boys looked at the wooden wall from top to bottom. There was no hole or crack on Benny's side.

The boys ran back to Rory's closet. They found a small crack and a loose board, but no room to run any rope through.

"Do you suppose we could make a hole?" Rory asked. "Would Granda Alden mind?"

Benny laughed and said, "No, he won't mind. But why do you say Granda Alden?"

"Well," answered Rory, "we say Granda in the part of Canada I come from. It's natural for me to say Granda, just as you say Grandfather."

The two boys raced down to the cellar and raced back with a saw, a hammer, and other tools. They made so much noise that Henry came up to see what was going on.

"We're going to rig a telegraph," Benny explained. "But we will have to cut out a piece of the closet to get the rope through."

"How will you work this, Ben?" Henry asked.

Benny said, "Well, this is how we think it will work. We will hang something like a piece of iron on each end of the rope. If I pull the rope on my side, there will be a knock on Rory's side."

Rory added, "It will be a telegraph because we will have signals. One knock means, 'Are you awake?' Then the answer can be two knocks for yes."

"We don't need a signal for no," Benny said. "If there's no answer, Rory is asleep."

Henry laughed. He said, "I'll ask Grandfather if he is willing to have you cut that hole. If I don't come right back and let you know, you can go ahead."

No one came to stop them. The boys succeeded in

cutting a very rough round hole through the double wood. It was a bigger hole than they needed, big enough to poke a finger or almost a hand through.

Next, the boys hunted for a rope to run through the hole. They found two old iron hooks in the tool chest. Rory tied one to the end of a rope in his room. Benny did the same thing with the other in his room.

Before the boys knew it, several hours had passed.

"There!" said Rory. "There is a fine telegraph to use tomorrow morning."

The boys called Mrs. McGregor to come up to see their new invention. She had heard the noise and was worried that Rory was doing some damage to the house.

She said, "Rory, I thought you were pounding this house down. You must remember this is not your house." Then she admired the new telegraph with its loud bangs. But soon she said, "Benny, Rory has not seen the rest of the house yet, or the yard."

So Benny and Rory walked all around the house and tried out the bicycles. Rory knew how to ride because at home he had to ride a bike to school.

Jeffrey and Sammy Beach, who lived next door to the Aldens, were gone for the summer. But Benny and Rory went up the ladder to see the tree house the Aldens had built with some help from their neighbors.

At dinner, Rory said, "Granda Alden, there seems to be a picture of this house in my room. It looks like a photograph."

"That is just what it is, Rory," replied Mr. Alden. "It is a photograph."

"And there's a family coming down the front walk," continued Rory. "It looks like a father and mother and their little girl."

"Just right again, my boy," said Mr. Alden, smiling. "You seem to want to know everything."

"That I do!" agreed Rory. "Do you know who the people are?"

"Yes, I do," answered Mr. Alden. "That is the family who lived here before I bought the house. You see I lived on this same street, not far away. I didn't know the people in this house very well. Their name was Shaw, and the child's name was Stephanie. Mr. Shaw sold me this house, and they all went to France to live. I have never heard from them since. Maybe someone else has, but I haven't. I paid them for the house, and that's all there was to it."

"Then the picture of the pretty little girl is Stephanie Shaw?" insisted Rory.

"That's right," said Mr. Alden again.

"But our house looks so funny," Benny objected. "The front door and the porch are the same, though."

Grandfather nodded. "That is because I had rooms added to the house to make it bigger. The work took a long time. It was nearly a year before the house was ready and I could move in."

"Was there any trouble?" asked Rory. "I mean between you and the Shaw family?"

Grandfather thought a minute. Then he said, "No, not exactly trouble. I did think the Shaws could have written to me from France."

"That is a little sad," Jessie said.

"It was almost as if the Shaws had never lived here at all," Mr. Alden said. "After a time everyone forgot that this had been the Shaw house once. It seemed as if it was always the Alden house."

Mrs. McGregor brought the dessert in. "That's right," she said. "It's been the Alden house for years now."

"And yet," Violet said, "little Stephanie called it home. I do wonder what happened to her."

"I suppose it will always be a mystery," Rory said.

"Maybe," Benny added. "With us you never know."

CHAPTER 3

Surprise from the Past

The next morning it was raining very hard. The sky was filled with black clouds.

"It's teeming," said Rory.

"It's pouring," said Benny. "We can't play outdoors very well."

"That's OK," Rory said. "We can work some more on our telegraph."

As the boys worked, Rory had an idea. He said, "We made that hole pretty big, Ben. Maybe we could pass messages through it."

Benny looked at the hole. He said, "Yes, I think we could. Let's make the hole a little bigger. If I knock three times, it means I've tied a message around the rope. Then you can pull it over to your side."

The boys tried out the new idea right away. But they ran into trouble.

"Ouch!" Rory exclaimed. "The rope is stuck. Look, this hole is full of splinters."

"I tell you what we can do, Rory," said Benny. "Let's make the hole square and sand the edges. It will be all right with Grandfather."

"Let's do that," Rory agreed. "We'll need the tools."

"That's easy," replied Benny. "We'll just go down to the cellar and get the tools again."

The boys picked out a short saw, a steel plane, a pair of pliers, and some sandpaper. Then they raced upstairs again.

"Don't you ever walk, Rory?" Jessie asked, laughing. She was going upstairs to her room.

"No, I don't walk when I can run," answered Rory. "What's the use of waiting around?" And by that time he was out of sight.

Mrs. McGregor said, "I do hope Rory isn't doing anything he shouldn't."

"No, he isn't," answered Henry. "I've watched the boys. They are just going to make a larger hole between their rooms through the closet wall. It's all right."

Rory was busy sawing the round hole into a square one. "Lots more room, Ben, to let the rope through. And it will look better, too, when we begin to smooth it off."

"Let me sandpaper," said Benny. "When I get tired, I'll hand it over to you."

Benny went to work. Then in a few minutes Rory took his turn.

It was not long before their arms were tired. It was hard work smoothing off the oak wood.

"We can rest a while," said Rory. "Did you notice that the wooden wall is double? There's quite a space between the two walls."

Benny said, "Yes, there's a grand little hidey-hole between these boards. If anyone wanted to hide a paper or a letter, nobody would ever find it."

"Who could hide a paper there?" said Rory. "Girls don't hide papers."

"Oh, don't they!" exclaimed Benny. "My sisters had a time when they hid the strangest things."

"Look if you want to," said Rory. "You might find an old will or something. I read about somebody finding a will in a mystery story. That would be exciting!"

"My fingers won't go in that space," said Benny after trying for a minute. "My hand is too big."

"Make your fingers as flat as you can," directed Rory. "You might at least touch something."

"No," said Benny at last. "You try. Your hand is smaller."

Benny came out of the clothes closet and Rory

went in. He made his fingers as flat as he could and slipped them into the space.

"I can't feel a thing," he said.

"Nothing at all?" Benny asked. "I just feel that there must be something there."

Rory made one last try, moving his fingers as much as he could.

"Oh, Ben!" he cried, "I do feel something! There's something in here."

"What does it feel like? Paper?" asked Benny.

"Not paper. It feels like cloth. But I simply can't get it between my fingers," said Rory.

"Here, try the pliers. Take your fingers out. The pliers are longer and thinner," said Benny.

"But what if I drop them?" Rory said.

"Let me tie a string on them first," said Benny. "Like this."

Then both boys held their breath as the long, slim pliers went into the slot.

"I've got something, Ben!" shouted Rory after several tries.

"Well, pull!" commanded Benny. "Try and pull it out, Rory. What could be in there?"

Rory twisted the pliers this way and that. He twisted his face the same way, too. He was a comical looking sight. But Benny did not laugh.

Then very slowly Rory drew out the pliers holding something strange made of thin blue cloth.

"What in the world is it?" asked Rory, holding it up by the pliers. "It's but a wee bit of cloth."

Benny answered, "I haven't the slightest idea."

The boys smoothed the cloth out on the floor and found it was old and torn in some places. But across the cloth in neat rows were bands of darker blue cloth sewed on very carefully by hand with odd uneven stitches.

The stitching seemed to make a row of little pockets. It was a big puzzle.

Benny turned the cloth over. He looked at the back and ran his finger along the stitches. What could this be for? Who could have made it? And why was it hidden between the closet walls?

Rory looked at the cloth, too. For once he did not find a thing to say.

At last Benny said, "I can guess just two things about this. It's been hidden for a long time. It must have been important to the person who made it."

"How do you know?" asked Rory.

"Because someone took the trouble to hide it," Benny said. "Oh, I wish I knew what it was for."

Jessie walked past the door and the boys called, "See what we found, Jessie!"

Jessie turned the cloth over and looked at it for a while. She said, "Looks like a man's sewing. No woman ever sewed like that."

"But what in the world is it?" Rory asked.

"I don't know," said Benny. "But Grandfather might. This thing was surely hidden or we wouldn't have found it in such a funny place. Nobody would look for anything pushed down between the boards."

"I'd dote on knowing what it is," Rory said.

"Grandfather will know," said Benny. "He knows just about everything. I'll ask him at dinnertime."

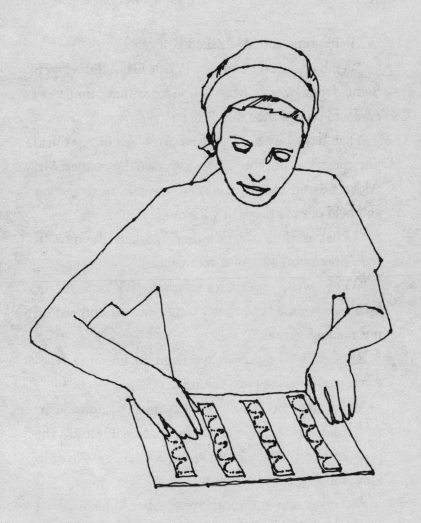

"What time is that?" asked Rory.

"Well, at different times. When Grandfather gets home from work, Mrs. McGregor has dinner all ready to put on the table."

That day, however, before Mrs. McGregor had put the meal on the table, the two boys met Mr. Alden's car at the driveway. They ran up to the car and held out the piece of blue cloth.

"What is this, Grandfather?" asked Benny. "It won't take you a second to answer."

"Well, well," said Grandfather. "What's all the hurry? Give me time to get out of the car and put on my reading glasses."

Rory said, "I suppose we want to know fast because we are so curious, Granda."

Mr. Alden and the boys went into the house. Mr. Alden sat down and put on his glasses. He took the piece of cloth. Jessie, Henry, and Violet came over to look, too.

After turning the cloth over, Mr. Alden said, "I really don't know for sure, boys, but I rather think this is a coin case. It is certainly old. Where in the world did you find it?"

"Rory found it," answered Benny. "It was hidden in a space between the walls of his clothes closet and the closet in my room."

Jessie said, "My guess is that Stephanie Shaw made it. The boys showed it to me. How old was she when she lived here, Grandfather?"

"She was about ten, I think."

Jessie shook her head. "A girl of ten ought to know how to sew better than that—at least in the days when every little girl *had* to sew."

"Not so fast, my dear," returned Mr. Alden. "Wait until you hear the whole story."

"Do you know the story of this cloth?" Henry asked, surprised.

"I will tell you all I know," replied his grandfather, "if you can all sit still and listen."

"Oh," said Rory, "listening is the best thing I do."

This made everyone laugh, even Rory, for he was always talking.

"I'll begin with that picture in Rory's room," Grandfather said. "That is a picture of the family that you know lived in this very house. They all moved to France, as I told you, and we never heard from any of them. The little girl's name was Stephanie Shaw. She was the most beautiful child I ever saw. And she was as good as she was beautiful."

"Just like a fairy princess," said Benny.

"Exactly!" said Grandfather, very much pleased. "She always made me think of a fairy princess. Her life was sad, though. Her father had special ideas about how she should grow up. He would not let her play with other children. He bought her everything she wanted, but she wanted some friends."

"Poor little rich girl," Jessie said.

"Yes, Jessie," replied Grandfather, "that's exactly how it was. Stephanie had beautiful clothes—but no friends her own age. Her mother had already gone to France to live when I met Stephanie. Perhaps Mr. Shaw was not sure how to treat a little girl."

"So you really didn't know her, did you?" asked

Violet. She felt sure her grandfather might have done something for Stephanie if anyone could.

"No, I didn't," Mr. Alden said. "But I knew about her because of my friend Professor Nichols. He saw a lot of Mr. Shaw and Stephanie. In fact, Professor Nichols and the little girl had the same hobby."

"What was it?" asked Rory, smiling. "Certainly not sewing!"

"No, not sewing," said Grandfather. "Something much more exciting than that."

"Please tell us," Violet begged. "I almost feel as if I've known Stephanie."

"The hobby was coin collecting," Mr. Alden said. "Even today Professor Nichols is the person to ask if you have any questions about coins. In those days, he knew a lot about coins. His hobby then was nickels."

Benny threw back his head and laughed. He said, "That's funny! Professor Nichols liked nickels."

"That's really funny, Ben," said Rory. "Nichols and nickels."

Mr. Alden spoke again. "Mr. Shaw thought it was

good for Stephanie to have a special interest like coins. He bought coins for her. It was Stephanie's idea to get some blue material to make cases to hold her collection. She and Professor Nichols called it the Blue Collection."

"But there are no coins here," Rory said. "Just the case."

"I wonder what happened," Benny said. "Maybe Stephanie took the coins with her when she went to France."

Grandfather shook his head. "Andrew Nichols didn't think so. He thought she left the collection somewhere in the house. You see, Stephanie thought she would be coming back. But she didn't."

"Why didn't the professor write to her and offer to send her the Blue Collection?" Henry asked.

"That's easy to answer," Mr. Alden said. "He didn't know her address."

Jessie laughed. "Well, that is a pretty good reason. Rory and Benny found only the empty coin case. Maybe the coins in the Blue Collection were stolen.

Then again, maybe the boys didn't search deep enough."

Benny and Rory looked at each other. They were both thinking of the small hole in the closet wall.

"That hole isn't very deep, Ben," said Rory. "Perhaps the coins are still there! We were so excited to find *anything* that we stopped looking when we found the cloth case."

The boys raced upstairs followed by all the Aldens, even Grandfather. Benny rushed into the closet while everyone stood still outside. They were wondering if Benny would find anything else hidden behind the wall.

CHAPTER 4

Is That All?

Rory held his breath as Benny reached into the hole in the closet wall. Benny was so excited that he almost let the pliers fall into the hole.

"Paper!" he said. "Hear it rustle?"

"Don't tear it, Benny," said Rory. "It must be very old."

"There's a lot of it," Benny said. By now he was able to touch the paper with his fingers. "It feels like a book without a cover."

"Pull it out!" Rory said.

"Here, you try," Benny replied. "It's not as easy as you think."

"I'll try," said Rory. "But it's in your house and it belongs to you, whatever it is."

Rory took the pliers and got a good grip on the papers. Out came a notebook without any cover. It was bent and wrinkled. The paper looked yellowed and old.

The two boys moved into the light. Benny held the papers out for Grandfather and the others to see. He said, "Homemade! Poor Stephanie! She had to make her own book."

"But what kind of book is it?" asked Violet.

Three rusty pins held together four pieces of school paper folded twice.

"Don't open it, Ben," said Rory. "Let's give it to Granda just as it is."

Mr. Alden was very careful with the paper book. He sat down at a table in Rory's room.

On the first page he read in big printing, MY JOURNAL BY STEPHANIE. Inside, the writing was something like an old lady's and also like a small child's.

"Please read what it says," Jessie said.

"Yes," Benny said. "Maybe there's a clue about the Blue Collection."

So Mr. Alden read what had been written so long ago. Rory and the others listened. They tried to imagine the little girl in her room, writing slowly about herself.

"I am ten years old and I think I should start a journal. I will never show it to anybody, so I can write what I choose.

"To begin with, I have dark brown curly hair and brown eyes. I look like my father, and I like the things he likes. My mother loves to go to parties in pretty clothes. I don't go to parties.

"Once my father and mother and I started to

church. A man with a camera came along and took our picture. My father wanted the picture. He bought it and I had it framed to surprise him.

"Now a journal has to know everything. I do not go to school, but my father has a teacher for me. I do not have any playmates, so my father helps me with a collection of coins. I made the case of blue cloth because I like blue. The sewing is not very good because nobody ever taught me how and I just picked it up, and besides I wasn't ten when I began.

"My father gave me some money and I bought the blue cloth from Miss Rachel. She is a very young woman, but she has a little shop and sells all kinds of things like cloth and pins and needles. I can talk to Miss Rachel. She's my friend.

"But I like to collect coins. I am always looking around for different coins. Sometimes Miss Rachel watches for a special penny I want, or a nickel or dime. My father gives me coins, too.

"I used to have five dolls. But now I am older, and I have given them away. Sometimes I wish I had them back, especially my baby doll with the long clothes and silk socks. I used to think she was real because she shut her eyes. I wish I hadn't thought I was too old for dolls. But I suppose coins take the place of dolls as one grows older. Anyway, I still have my dollhouse for little dolls.

"I hope that when I grow up I shall write a wonderful book like *Heidi* and everybody will read it. I can do that and collect coins, too.

"My father said to me, Stephanie, you are a very smart little girl. Why don't you think up some kind of hard puzzle that nobody can solve? Then hide it somewhere. So that is what I am going to do, a puzzle with hard clues and everything.

"I think I can make up a puzzle that nobody can solve, not even my father. I will make it easy at first and that will fool him."

Mr. Alden stopped and looked around.

"Don't stop," Benny said. "Go on."

"That's all," Mr. Alden said. "I have read it all to you. There is nothing more."

Jessie said, "Well, it does sound like a little girl's diary. I wrote some things like that once, too."

"Oh, dear!" said Rory. "I thought we were going to learn some great secret about the house and my room."

"So did I, Rory," said Mr. Alden with a rather sad smile.

"What shall we do with the journal?" Benny asked. "It won't do any good to put it back where it came from."

Violet said, "Let me keep it. I'll put it in a safe place."

Grandfather handed Violet the papers held together with the rusty pins. Then he went downstairs.

Rory said, "I guess we can put the pliers away. We won't need them."

Benny nodded. "There isn't any use in looking for the coins in the wall. I'm sure someone found them and stole them, just the way Jessie said."

"But we can't be certain the coins were stolen," Rory said. "I don't think they were. I think those coins are still hidden someplace. But what good is that if we can't find them?"

Benny said, "Well, let's think for a minute. How did Stephanie put the things in the wall in the first place?"

"She didn't saw a hole the way we did," Rory said.

"No, I'm sure she didn't do that," Benny said. "Let's take another look."

So Benny got his flashlight again and both boys began to look carefully at the back wall of Rory's closet.

The wall was made of narrow boards fitted together. Small nails held the boards in place.

Suddenly Benny said, "Look, Rory!" and pointed to a place where a nail was missing. The empty nail hole was easy to see. And the nail at the other end of the board was very loose.

Rory ran his finger around the small nail. It wiggled a bit, just like a loose tooth. He tried to pull the nail out, but it was a little rusty.

"Here," Benny said. "Use the pliers to hold the

head of the nail. Maybe if you try that it will come out."

And the nail did! After that it was easy to pull the narrow board away. There was the empty space that held the coin case and the sheets of the journal Stephanie had written. The hiding place was near enough to the hole the boys had made to let them reach into it.

Benny looked thoughtfully at the loose board. He said, "I guess Stephanie must have discovered this hiding place and decided to use it for a secret place of her own."

"And somebody else found it and took out the coins," said Benny. "Too bad."

"I tell you what we can do," said Rory. "Let's look all around my room before we go to dinner."

Benny began to smile. He said, "You are right, Rory. If a board was loose in the closet, maybe there's some other hiding place."

The boys got down on their hands and knees. They began to crawl along the floor, looking for a loose board.

"Can we roll up the rug?" Rory asked.

"Sure," Benny said.

But there were no loose boards.

"We could see if anyone had nailed a loose board down," Benny said thoughtfully. "I think the nail would be different. But how about under the bed, Rory?"

"It's probably all dusty," Rory said.

Benny laughed. "You don't know Mrs. McGregor then! Come on, help me push the bed over. You'll see."

"It's more fun to crawl under the bed," Rory said. "Hold up the edge of the spread."

"Here we go," Benny said.

Pretty soon there were two pairs of boys' shoes sticking out from under the bed.

"See anything?" Benny asked.

"Not even dust," Rory said. "You're right about Mrs. McGregor."

"No dust, no sneezes," Benny said. "And no hiding place for coins, either."

The boys crawled back out from under the bed.
They stood up and stretched.

"Where else shall we look?" Rory asked.

"I think the furniture is new," Benny said. "At
least I think Grandfather had it put in here."

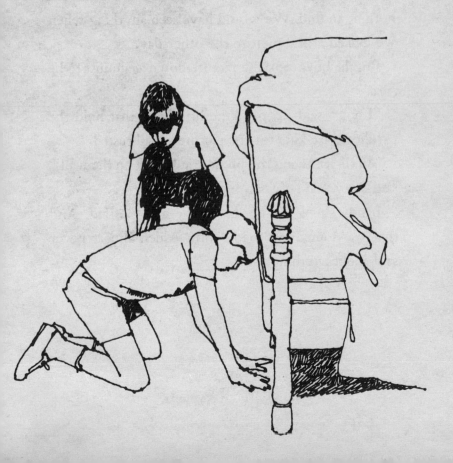

"But what about the picture?" Rory asked. "That is old."

Benny said, "You're right. Maybe there's a secret place in the wall behind the picture."

Rory went over and looked. Then he said, "Oh, Benny, you're trying to fool me! You know there is nothing to find. We would have seen anything when we looked at the picture the other day."

But the boys took the picture down again just to be sure.

"Look," said Benny, "the little nails that hold the cardboard backing for the picture are all rusted."

"Well, let's hang the photograph back on the wall," said Rory. "Where can we look now?"

Benny shook his head. "I give up," he said. And that was something that Benny Alden almost never said about anything.

CHAPTER 5

A New Clue

Violet came to the door of Rory's room. She had put Stephanie's journal away. It was time to call Benny and his guest to dinner.

"What's wrong?" she asked. "You two boys look as if you haven't a friend in the world."

Benny said, "We thought maybe Stephanie had some other hiding places in her room. But we can't find a thing."

"Not even any dust under the bed," Rory said.

"Well, it was a long time ago," Violet said. "I'm not surprised. But dinner is ready. Maybe you'll have some ideas later."

But no one had any new ideas even though they talked about the mystery at dinner.

Jessie said, "I wonder who Miss Rachel was. Do you suppose she's still living in Greenfield?"

"I guess she'd be an old lady now," Benny said.

Mr. Alden smiled at Benny and Rory. "Why don't you boys go for a bike ride and forget about mysteries?" he asked. So the boys did that.

But the next morning Rory and Benny began to think about hidden coins again.

The boys stood around in Rory's room.

Suddenly Benny said, "Rory! There might be something we missed." He rushed back to the closet.

Rory stared. He didn't have any idea what Benny meant.

"Let's push the clothes out of the way," Benny said. "Now where's that loose board? Here it is."

Rory watched while Benny poked his fingers up into the space. The boys had already looked in the space below the hole. But they hadn't tried to reach up. Now Benny was reaching upward instead of downward.

Henry came in Rory's room just then. "Need help?" he asked.

"Ouch!" Benny said. "I've hurt my finger. Something got under my fingernail."

"Be more careful," Henry said.

"Something's up there where I can just reach it," Benny said. "Something with a sharp corner, I'd guess."

Before anyone could stop him, Benny was trying again to move his fingers around in the small opening. All at once he touched something.

"It's a little card!" Benny exclaimed as he pulled a small piece of cardboard out of the wall.

"A card," said Rory. "Is anything written on it?"

"Don't rush me," said Benny, breathing hard. "I have to get the card in the light."

Rory and Henry crowded around Benny. They all looked at the card. The message written on it said, "Ask Miss Rachel for blue cloth."

"That's Stephanie's writing," Benny said. "It's like the writing in the journal."

Henry said, "Maybe she wrote that to remind herself to buy the cloth for the coin case."

Benny read the message again. He shook his head. "I don't think she would write a message to herself. She would remember that cloth."

"Yes, she would," Rory agreed.

"Does the card have anything on the other side?" Henry asked.

Benny turned it over. "Something was written and erased," Benny said. "I can't read it."

Henry asked for the card and looked at it. He shook his head.

"Let me look at the card again," Benny said, holding out his hand.

He looked at the front, then he turned the card over. He walked to the desk in Rory's room and sat down. He pulled open a drawer and took out a pencil.

"What are you going to do?" Rory asked.

"Watch," Benny said. He scribbled over the card with the pencil, working very lightly.

As the others looked over his shoulder, they saw the outline of white letters begin to show.

"See?" Benny said. "Stephanie pressed hard when she wrote on this side of the card. She erased the writing, but the hard strokes stayed. I think we can read what she wrote."

"You're right," Henry exclaimed.

Soon Benny read slowly, "L.S. First clue. Go to 5 Birds."

For a moment the boys were too surprised to talk. Then Henry said, "The words 'First clue' sound like a puzzle. Didn't Stephanie say she was going to make a puzzle?"

Benny said, "L.S. Now what could that mean?"

Rory spoke up. "I have an idea. I think the S. is for Shaw. Now I wonder about that L. Let's ask Granda. He's still home."

When Grandfather looked at the letters he said, "Yes, I think the S. stands for Shaw. Stephanie's father was named Leland Shaw. That would be your L.S."

"That's right!" Benny exclaimed. "Stephanie wrote in her journal that she was going to make a puzzle for her father. He told her to make up a puzzle, and she thought he might as well play, too. Her father isn't around to get this note, so now the clue is meant for us. That's what I think."

"Well," agreed Henry, "let's try it."

"You know what this reminds me of?" said Benny. "It reminds me of an old game we used to play, a treasure hunt."

"We have treasure hunts in Canada," Rory said. "I know what you mean. Somebody hides a treasure but gives the hunters a note saying 'Look in the hole in the oak tree.' Then the players look in that hole and find another note. No treasure. Just a note that says 'Look under the cushion in the porch rocker.'"

Benny interrupted, "Then there is another note

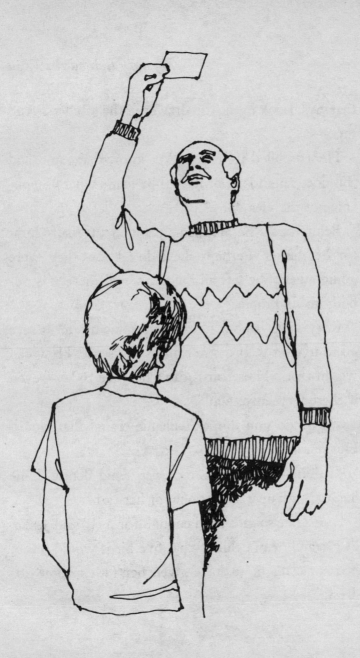

that says 'Look in the top drawer in the kitchen.' And then—"

Henry smiled at Benny. "We know that game, and this does remind me of it. Maybe that's where Stephanie got the idea."

Benny said, "So Stephanie planned a treasure hunt for her father. Perhaps she didn't know they were going away. She left all the notes, and there was nobody to find them."

Rory said, "But what does this clue mean? It says go to five birds. It doesn't make any sense. How can we do that? Those birds can't be alive today—even if there were any then."

"Why do you think Stephanie erased that clue?" Henry asked.

"I think the clue was too easy," said Benny. "She had to think up a harder one for her father."

"This one sounds hard enough for me," said Jessie. "I certainly can't think what five birds would mean. Stephanie ought to have given her father some address."

"Hey!" said Henry suddenly. "That's just what this is—an address!"

"You might be right, Henry," said Jessie. "Five birds. It does sound like an address."

"Well, suppose it is an address," said Benny. "I've never heard of it. Greenfield is such a small town, and I thought I knew every street in it."

"But I think I have seen it, Ben," Henry said thoughtfully. "One day when I was riding my bike, I was looking for a shortcut across town. Well, I turned into a short, narrow street that had only two stores on it. I think the street was called Birds Lane. I remember the name because it was so different and because one of the stores was called the Wren Shop. The Wren Shop and Birds Lane go together, so it is easy to remember."

The family agreed, laughing.

Suddenly Grandfather said, "Possibly you can find your Miss Rachel there, even if the name is Wren."

"You know something, Granda!" exclaimed Rory.

"You know something we don't. What is it?"

"Go and see for yourself," said Mr. Alden. "You all need exercise." And with that, Mr. Alden would not say more.

"Well, let's find Violet, and we'll all ride our bikes to the other side of town," said Jessie. "We have to look for Birds Lane."

Rory and Benny ran to find Violet. The boys explained about the clue on the little card.

Violet said, "Wait a minute, Benny. Don't be in such a big hurry. What blue cloth do you think Stephanie meant?"

Jessie said, "I'd guess the same kind of cloth she used for the coin cases. But I can't imagine anyone would have any of that left. It was years ago."

Benny shook his head. "I know. But it won't do any harm to go and see where 5 Birds Lane is. Maybe someone will remember Miss Rachel. We can try."

Rory added, "It's the only clue we have. We have to try it."

Violet said, "If Stephanie meant that special blue

cloth, let's take the coin case along. Just in case we need it. I'll get it."

In a very short time the Aldens and Rory were pedaling down the broad main street of Greenfield. They looked at every street sign, hoping to find Birds Lane.

It was a beautiful day, and not too hot to enjoy a long bike ride across town. But none of the children were thinking about the pleasant ride. Every one of them was thinking about old money, money made of copper and silver, brass and tin.

CHAPTER 6

Jenny Wren

It did not take the Aldens and Rory very long to get to the other side of town. But once they got there, Henry did not find his way so easily. This was the older section of Greenfield, and the children had not been there very often.

Henry led the way and the others followed, up one narrow street and down another.

"We'll never find it," said Rory.

"Oh, yes we will!" said Benny. "We'll find Birds Lane if it takes all day."

Suddenly Henry called out, "Wait! I think we are close by. Look at that big old house with its windows boarded up. I remember seeing that before. I think Birds Lane is only a block or two ahead."

Benny raced up the street ahead of the others. When he got to the corner, he hopped off his bike. He called out, "You are right, Henry. Here it is. The street sign says Birds Lane."

Benny waited for everyone to catch up, and then he started down the narrow street. The first address he saw was 3 Birds Lane. It was a doctor's office. Then came 5 Birds Lane.

"Why, look at that sign!" Violet exclaimed. "It's the Jenny Wren Shop. What fun to have a name like that on Birds Lane!"

In a minute the Aldens were opening a door to a shop filled with yarn, cloth, and all sorts of sewing supplies.

A young woman smiled at the children and asked, "What can I do for you?"

Jessie and Violet had been looking all around the tiny shop. But now Violet stepped to the counter and said, "We've come for some special blue cloth, like this." She took out the coin case.

The young woman picked up the coin case. She looked at it curiously.

"I've never seen anything like this," she said. "No one has had cloth like that for a long time."

Jessie said, "That's true. We think this is about forty years old, at least."

"Wait here," the young woman said. "I'd like to show this to someone. Is that all right with you?"

The Aldens nodded, and the young woman disappeared through a door at the back of the shop. Soon she came back and a small older lady was with her. She had white hair and she walked a little slowly.

The young woman said, "Aunt Rachel, these are the children who brought this blue cloth in. Maybe they can tell you where it came from."

Benny said, "Excuse me, but are you Miss Rachel?"

The lady smiled and said, "Yes, I am, but I haven't been called that for years. I'm Mrs. Wren now. This is my niece, Jenny Wren."

But Benny was still bothered. He said, "You did have a shop here one time in the past, didn't you?"

Mrs. Wren answered, "Yes, I did. I just called it 'Number 5 Birds Lane.' I sold cloth and thread and needles to everyone in Greenfield."

"Then—then do you remember a little girl named Stephanie Shaw?" Benny asked, almost holding his breath.

"Oh, indeed I do!" Mrs. Wren's voice was trembling. "Poor little thing! She would be fifty years old by now—if she had lived. Did you know that she had died?"

"No, we didn't. How sad," replied Jessie. "Our grandfather is James Alden. Perhaps you know him?"

"Oh, yes," said Mrs. Wren quickly. "Mr. Alden is a fine gentleman. Of course he doesn't come to the shop, but Mrs. McGregor comes to buy dish towels and we talk together. I know that Mr. Alden bought the Shaw house long ago."

Benny said, "We found this coin case hidden in our house. And we found a note Stephanie Shaw wrote that said 'Ask Miss Rachel for blue cloth.' But I guess it doesn't do any good. You don't have that cloth anymore."

Mrs. Wren said, "Little Stephanie did buy that blue cloth from me to make cases for coins. She loved to come in and talk to me. Of course I was just a young woman then."

"Did you hear from her after she went to France?" asked Jessie.

"Oh, yes, she wrote the loveliest letters. She would have been a writer if she had lived. I'm sure of that. She and her family died in a railroad accident—there was no one left. But oh, I am so glad you came in. You don't know!"

"Why?" asked Benny, smiling. "Three boys and two girls to buy half a yard of cloth that you don't even have."

"I'll show you," Mrs. Wren said. She took down an old-fashioned sewing box and opened it. There were old buttons, some bits of lace, and scraps of yarn. She took out a folded piece of paper and gave it to Jessie. "That's why," she said.

The paper was yellow with age. Jessie unfolded it carefully. She read aloud "Give this note to anybody who comes in to buy blue cloth for a coin collection. S.S."

"Now, what do you think of that?" Benny said in amazement. "And you kept this all these years?"

Mrs. Wren smiled a little. She said, "Well, I really loved that pretty child. I kept this just to remind me of her. Old ladies do things like that, you know."

Rory said, "But that can't be all. There must be more of a message."

"Look on the back," said Mrs. Wren.

Jessie turned the paper over and read, "Attic, dollhouse."

"Does that mean anything to you?" asked Mrs. Wren. "I've read it a hundred times. I didn't know

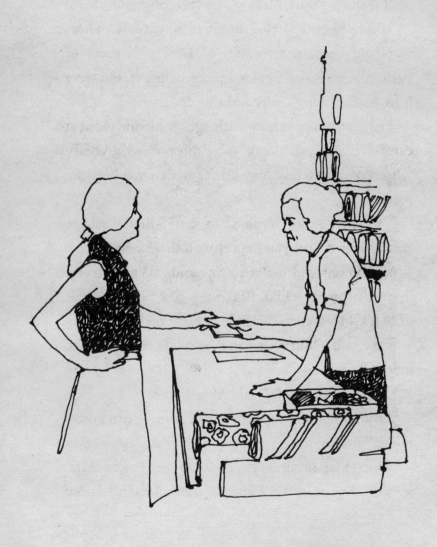

who was ever coming in nor what Stephanie meant about a dollhouse."

"Oh, it means something, all right," Benny answered. "You see, Stephanie really had a fine coin collection and it's been lost. She hid it somewhere. Some people thought it was stolen. We hope to find it."

"This may be the clue we need," Jessie said. "Oh, it's so lucky you saved this piece of paper all these years."

Benny was nearest to the shop door. He looked as if he were going to run out.

"Thank you!" he said. "Thank you, Mrs. Wren!"

Mrs. Wren and her niece smiled. "I know you want to get back and explore the attic," the white-haired lady said. "I understand. Do let us know if you find anything."

"We will," Violet promised.

The Aldens left the little sewing shop and got on their bikes. They headed toward the street that would take them back to their own neighborhood.

"I hope we find Stephanie's dollhouse in the attic," Jessie said as she rode along. "But I can't remember seeing a dollhouse up there."

"The attic has a lot of dark corners," Henry told her.

Benny said, "It would be just too bad if we had this much of Stephanie's puzzle and never found the coins at all."

Rory said, "Ben, that just can't happen. We have to find the Blue Collection."

"On with the hunt!" Benny shouted and raced all the others home.

CHAPTER 7

A Real Puzzle

Rory looked puzzled as he rode along with the Aldens on their bikes.

"What's the matter?" said Jessie.

"How do you get up to your attic?" asked Rory. "I don't remember any stairs to an attic."

Benny heard Rory's question. He said, "The attic stairs are behind a narrow door."

"That's why you didn't know about the attic," Jessie said. "We never go up there."

When they reached home, they put their bikes away and ran straight upstairs to the narrow door to the attic. Jessie opened the door and they began to climb.

"The stairs are steep," said Rory. "Oh, what a dark place! I suppose those are just shadows over by the chimney, Ben?"

"Yes, they're only shadows," replied Benny. "This place looks spooky enough to have any number of clues. We'll really have to look."

"You're brave, Ben," said Rory. "I would never come up here alone. That's sure."

"Neither would I," said Benny. "I haven't been up here for years."

The attic had only two windows, one at each end. They didn't do much good. It was very dim in the attic, and there were no electric lights to turn on.

"Let's start by the chimney," said Henry. "There isn't much up here after all."

"Now wouldn't you know that!" exclaimed Jessie. "An attic is always supposed to be full of junk and old chairs and things. It's almost empty up here."

"Probably Grandfather had a grand clearing out," Henry suggested. "I hope no one threw away my old electric train. I'd like to have it for the sake of old times."

"Come here, Henry," called Benny from behind the chimney. "Here's a box with your electric train. It's on the floor."

Violet said, "Oh, Benny, we don't care about the train. We want to find Stephanie's dollhouse. Where can it be?"

"Wait!" Benny called. "It's so dark back here I can't see much. But I just think maybe I've found something else."

Jessie said, "It's almost too much to hope the next clue is still somewhere up here."

Benny called, "It *is* the dollhouse!"

Henry said, "The first thing is to move that dollhouse out into the light. Come on, Ben, help me."

Henry and Benny moved the wooden house out into the center of the attic. The light from one window fell on it.

The whole front of the dollhouse was open so that a little girl could play with it. She could walk the dolls from one room to another.

The house was dusty, and Jessie found an old cloth and wiped off the roof and the four little rooms.

When she dusted in the biggest room, Jessie stopped. She pulled something out and said, "This shoebox probably holds the furniture."

Violet took off the cover and found that Jessie was right. This was certainly Stephanie Shaw's doll furniture. Scraps of cloth from Miss Rachel's shop had been used to cover chairs and other pieces.

"Isn't this pretty?" said Jessie, holding up a tiny sofa covered with soft blue material.

"Yes," said Benny, who was not interested in furniture. "But what we want are coins—or another clue."

"Now, Ben, just be patient," said Rory. "We have

to do this little by little. If we don't we'll miss the clue. You take out the drawers from this dresser."

"Stephanie never made that," Benny replied, taking the piece of doll furniture. "Somebody bought this. It has the name of the toy company stamped right on the back. And I can't find anything that looks like a clue."

"Well, here is a toy clock," said Jessie. "It winds up and everything. Look, the key is still inside."

She took the key and wound the clock. The children were fascinated to hear the tiniest bell striking five.

They looked carefully at every piece of furniture and found nothing. They looked in all the small rooms and poked down the little wooden chimney. Henry even turned the dollhouse over to look under it.

"I was wrong about a clue here," Benny said. "There's nothing here. No note. No coins."

Suddenly it grew so dark in the attic that everyone had to give up.

"But only for today, Violet," promised Benny. "Tomorrow the hunt will go on."

But as it turned out, they did not go right up to the attic the next morning. Very early the Aldens' telephone rang.

Benny answered it and knew the voice right away. It was Mrs. Wren.

"Oh, yes, Mrs. Wren," Benny said. "It's not too early. Is there something special?"

Rory was standing near Benny. He put his hand over his mouth to keep from asking, "What is it?"

Benny was saying, "You want to see us? We'll come over on our bikes."

Then Mrs. Wren said something and Benny listened. He answered, "No, we didn't find anything in the attic. Nothing at all that helped us . . . Oh! You think so? . . . Yes, we'll have our breakfast first."

Benny waited while Mrs. Wren spoke, then he said, "Please don't talk that way, Mrs. Wren. You are not silly. You are very good to call us."

By this time the whole family was listening. As Benny said "Good-bye," Henry asked, "What is it, Ben?"

"Is something wrong?" Jessie asked.

"I don't know. Mrs. Wren is upset about something. She kept saying she was silly. 'A silly old woman' is what she said."

"Well," said Violet, "it must be something important or she would never have had the courage to call us so early."

Mr. Alden was already sitting at the breakfast table. He said, "I take it your Mrs. Wren wants to see you again."

"That's right, Grandfather," said Benny. "I can hardly eat."

Everyone smiled at that. Benny could always eat. But Rory didn't understand. He said, "You'd better eat, Ben. I can eat my breakfast all right."

So the bacon and eggs and toast disappeared.

In a short time Mr. Alden got up to leave for his office. The Aldens and Rory were starting out on their bicycles for the Jenny Wren Shop.

As soon as they came into the little store, Mrs. Wren greeted them. "Oh, I am sorry to bother you!" she said. "I shouldn't have called you so early."

Violet took Mrs. Wren's hand and said, "You aren't bothering us. I think you are the only person in town who can help us."

"I am getting so forgetful," Mrs. Wren said. "That's why I'm so glad my niece runs the shop for me now. But Jenny isn't here yet."

Benny was afraid that Mrs. Wren was forgetting why she had called. He held his breath.

But she went on, "I'm so forgetful, especially when I'm excited. And I was excited yesterday when you came and asked about the blue cloth. I was so surprised!"

"We understand," Jessie said quietly. "I'm sure you never thought anyone would ask for that little note left with you so long ago."

Mrs. Wren shook her head. "I had given up the idea long ago. And then when you did come, I forgot that I had another note."

"Another note?" Benny asked. He could hardly believe what he had heard.

"Yes, Stephanie left two notes with me. She told me to give the first one to the person who asked for the blue cloth. I was to give the second note when someone gave me a coat button."

Everyone looked surprised. Then Henry said, "I think I know. Stephanie probably had three or four treasure hunt clues. Like the one in the dollhouse that we couldn't find. Somehow that clue must have been lost."

Rory nodded his head and said, "Maybe another clue that said 'Take a button to Miss Rachel' was hidden somewhere."

"That's a good guess," Benny said. "But Mrs. Wren, you will let us have the second note, won't you?"

"Oh, yes, I have it right here," and Mrs. Wren gave Jessie a folded paper.

Jessie read in a clear voice, " 'Come on, Papa. Look on the back of the house. Outside, inside. Can't you solve my puzzle? Keep it if you wish.' "

Jessie looked up, frowning.

"That's just silly," Benny said quickly. "It doesn't sound like Stephanie or anybody else. It's just a bunch of words."

Nobody said anything. They all looked at Benny.

Soon he said doubtfully, "Maybe it isn't meant to say anything. Maybe . . ."

"Maybe what?" Rory demanded.

"Maybe it's a hidden message—a code."

"Now you're talking, Ben," said Henry. "That may be what it is."

Mrs. Wren had been looking at the children and listening. Now she said, "If it turns out to be a secret message, will you let me know? And tell me if you find the coins?"

"It's easy to promise that," said Jessie. "Of course we will let you know. If you hadn't saved these little notes all these years there would be no chance of finding the Blue collection."

"But we haven't found it yet," Henry said.

"We will," Benny said.

"Let's go back to your house and study the note," said Rory. "It has to mean something."

When the Aldens reached home, Violet said, "Let me copy that paper. If it is in plain printing it may look different to us."

"You're welcome to copy it," Benny said. "I still don't think it means much the way it is. Who could look on the back of a house?"

"What house?" Rory asked. "We looked all over that dollhouse. Nothing there."

Henry said slowly, "If it means the back of the house she lived in, we're out of luck. Grandfather had the house all changed. He added rooms at the back. Remember what he told us?"

Violet was busy copying the words. She had taken a stiff card and was printing in large letters with black ink. She put one sentence on each line. It made the words look quite different.

Benny read the words slowly,

"Come on, Papa!

Look on the back of the house.

Outside, inside.

Can't you solve my puzzle?

Keep it if you wish."

The Aldens looked at each other. It was true. The words did not make any sense.

Benny held the cardboard out as far from his eyes as he could. Then he shouted, "I have it! Just look at the first letters of the sentences! Read the first letters down." He laughed and handed the card back to Jessie.

"Of course," she said. "Now I see it. C-L-O-C-K, clock! The first letters spell clock. It is just as plain as it can be—if you know what you are looking for."

Everyone told Benny how smart he was.

"But what does clock mean?" asked Rory. "We looked at the dollhouse clock so many times that I can tell you every bump on the paint."

Jessie said, "I'm sure there's no clock belonging to the Shaws still in the house. Oh, dear! And I thought we were so close to finding the Blue Collection!"

Henry said, "Wait a minute, Jessie. Don't give up! We found Stephanie Shaw's dollhouse in the attic. Perhaps there's a little clock of hers up there, too."

Benny laughed, "Wouldn't it be fun if there was a cuckoo clock up there? And the little bird in the clock had a message for us? From Birds Lane!"

Henry said, "There's one way to find out. Let's look."

"Attic again," said Rory cheerfully.

They climbed the steep attic stairs. They looked around in the attic. It was so bare that once again the search seemed hopeless.

CHAPTER 8

So Near, So Far

The attic was dark and gloomy. The day was cloudy. Not much light came in through the small windows at each end of the attic.

"Where can we look?" asked Rory. "All I see is the dollhouse. And we know the dollhouse clock doesn't have a secret."

Benny just shook his head. It looked as if the treasure hunt had come to an end. The lost Blue Collection would never be found.

"What do you think, Jessie?" asked Henry. "I guess we might as well go downstairs."

But Jessie was looking hard at something. She said slowly, "When you found the dollhouse behind the chimney, was there anything else there?"

Benny said, "It was dark, but I think the dollhouse was the only thing."

"Well, I am going to feel behind the chimney," said Jessie. "If I can't see anything, perhaps I can feel something."

"You're more than welcome," replied Benny. "It's really too dark for me. I like to see what I'm touching."

Rory laughed at Benny and said, "There could be something scary. I read a story about a skeleton in an attic."

"Not in this attic," Benny said. "Mrs. McGregor would have swept it out."

Stepping carefully, Jessie moved toward the back of the big chimney. The shadows were very dark. She asked, "Rory, why do you have to talk about skeletons? I know there can't be one here. But it is scary."

"I'll look," Henry offered.

But Jessie said, "No, I'm here. Wait—"

Jessie put out her hand toward the back of the chimney. She did not touch bricks. She touched smooth wood.

"There is something back here!" Jessie exclaimed. "It's a piece of furniture or something tall and thin. Now what can it be?"

"Oh, I wish I had my flashlight," Benny said.

"I can feel carved wood and some glass," Jessie said. "And a little knob."

Jessie did her best to see what was hidden in the shadows. "Rory!" she called. "I've found something with a face and hands!"

"Bones?" asked Rory, and now he did not sound so brave.

"I'm sorry. I didn't mean to scare you, Rory,"

Jessie said. "I think there is a big clock here. A grand-father's clock."

"A real clock!" Benny said. "That has to be the clock Stephanie meant."

"Careful, Ben," Henry said. "It might be the clock. But don't count on it."

Jessie called, "It's too dark to see the clock back here. Henry, maybe you and Benny can move it."

She stepped back. The two boys carefully lifted the tall clock out into the small space were it was light.

Violet found the cloth they had used to dust the dollhouse and she dusted the old clock. It was really a handsome grandfather's clock.

"Now where would Stephanie hide a clue in a clock?" asked Jessie.

"In the back," Rory suggested. "She'd hide the clue where it wouldn't be seen."

"Yes," Henry said. "I don't suppose the clock was in the attic when Stephanie hid the clues for her treasure hunt."

There was a door on the back of the clock. Benny tried to open it, then Rory tried. At last Henry tried. He rattled the knob a little, and the door came open.

The Aldens and Rory all looked in the open space. It was a wonderful hiding place for a message. But it was empty.

"Oh," Benny said. "Someone else found the clue. Now we'll never know where Stephanie's treasure is."

Violet looked quietly at the old clock. She walked around to the front. She said, "I don't think a girl like Stephanie could have put anything in the back of the clock. She wouldn't have been able to move it. And if she did, I don't think she could have opened that door."

"That's so," Benny agreed. He too walked around the clock, looking at it from all sides.

Henry said, "I can open the glass door in front of the clock face. Stephanie could have reached it if she stood on a chair."

He opened the door and looked at the face and the

clock hands. He could see no message at all.

"What about the glass door where the pendulum is?" asked Benny.

Rory said, "Ben, you don't have to open it. You can just look in. I can't see a thing."

"Let's just open it anyway," Benny said. "I wonder if we need a key? No, it opens all right."

The big pendulum moved a little when Benny touched it carefully. Two heavy weights hung from chains.

"Could Stephanie have put some sort of message behind the weights?" Jessie asked.

"It's too dark to see," Rory said.

"I should go and get my flashlight," Benny said. "Come on, Rory, help me find it."

Henry said, "All right. You get the flashlight. We'll sit here on the attic stairs and tell ghost stories."

Jessie said, "Henry, don't make jokes. We really do want to find Stephanie's message—if there is one."

"I think it must be lost," Henry said. "Or maybe this isn't the right clock."

Rory and Benny were soon back with the flashlight.

"Stand back," Benny said. He flashed the light around the inside of the clock. Nothing.

"Benny!" Violet said. "Don't look in the clock. Shine your light on the door. I thought I saw something."

Benny shone the light on the inside of the door. Along the wooden frame the Aldens saw something folded. It was tacked to the inside of the door frame.

"See what it is," Benny said.

"Let me take the tacks out," Henry said. And in a moment he had the folded paper loose. He gave it to Violet. "See what it says," he told her.

Violet unfolded the paper and the Aldens stared. There was a message in large faded printing. It was surely done by Stephanie.

Violet read aloud, "This is the end. Look on the back of the house, but don't break the glass."

"What in the world!" shouted Benny. "What glass?"

"What house?" asked Jessie. "This house?"

"Or the dollhouse?" suggested Violet.

But Rory said, "We've looked the dollhouse over until I know every inch of it. Besides, it doesn't have any glass."

"That's so," Violet agreed. "And I'm sure Stephanie can't have meant the glass door in the front of the clock face. Let's go down to Rory's room and try to think. We haven't any more clues. This is the last one."

The children left the tall clock where it was and clattered down to Rory's room. Rory and Henry sat on the floor, but Benny made himself comfortable in a soft armchair. "Now let's think what Stephanie meant by the back of the house," Benny said. "This house?"

"Maybe this house," said Jessie. "The message says to look at the back of the house."

Violet shook her head. "It says 'on the back of the house.' That isn't quite the same thing."

Benny said, "Well, I think Jessie has the best idea

so far. Let's go out and look at the back of the house."

"I don't think it will do us much good," Henry said. "You have to think how long ago Stephanie left that clue. I can't see how it could still be on the back of the house."

"Perhaps so," Jessie agreed.

But Benny said, "You may be right, Henry. But if we go out and look, we might get some new ideas."

"I'll come too," Rory offered.

So the Aldens and Rory went downstairs and around to the back of the big house.

"Grandfather added the rooms on the back of the house after he bought it from the Shaws," Henry said. "I guess most of the back was changed."

"The part where the attic is wasn't changed," Benny said. "I'm sure of that."

They stared up at one of the small attic windows. " 'Don't break the glass,' " Rory said.

"Do you think Stephanie could have hidden the clue on the outside of the house near the attic window?" Benny asked.

"How could she do that?" Violet asked. "She'd have to crawl out of the window. She would never have done that."

"I guess that is true," Benny had to agree.

Violet said, "I have an idea. We have to try to think the way Stephanie did. Maybe we can guess where she hid that clue."

Jessie nodded. "I'm sure Stephanie must have chosen some place she could get to easily."

Rory said, "I think the clue must have been put inside the house somewhere. But perhaps it could be seen from the outside."

"Between the screen and the window glass," Violet suggested. "That would be easy for Stephanie to do."

"It would be too easy to find," Benny said. "Anybody could have found it. Violet, please read how the clue begins. I've forgotten."

Violet unfolded the paper and read, " 'This is the end.' "

"There," Benny said. "I think this must be the last clue. This clue should lead us to the place where the coins were hidden. If that's so, it had to be a safe place."

Henry shook his head. "Benny, the more I think about it, the more I think the Blue Collection will stay a mystery. Too bad."

"I guess so," Jessie said.

Even Violet said, "I have to give up, too."

Soon Rory and Benny found themselves alone behind the house. Everyone else had gone off to do something.

"Let's go back to my room," Rory suggested. "If we're going to think, we might as well be comfortable."

Up in Rory's room, Benny said, "Let me think. Coins aren't very big." He pulled a quarter, two dimes, a nickel, and four pennies out of his pocket. He made a little stack of them.

Rory said, "Stephanie had more coins than that."

"You're right," Benny said. "There are more pockets in the blue cloth coin case. But even that many coins wouldn't take up much room."

Benny and Rory stared at the coins. Where would a ten-year-old girl have thought of hiding a stack of coins?

"But what did she mean by 'on the back of the house' and 'don't break the glass'?" asked Benny.

"I give up," Rory said. "It's too much of a mystery for me."

"Well, I don't give up," Benny said. "I just need to think about something else for a while. Let's ride our bikes over to 5 Birds Lane and tell Mrs. Wren how close and how far we are from the collection."

"It's better than sitting here," Rory said.

CHAPTER 9

"Don't Break the Glass!"

When Benny and Rory walked into the Jenny Wren Shop they found Mrs. Wren watering some plants in the sunny shop window.

"Did you find the coin collection?" she asked. "Oh! I can see by the look on your faces that you didn't."

Benny said, "But we did find the next clue. It was inside the grandfather's clock, up in our attic."

"It doesn't help us at all," Rory said. "Stephanie wrote to look on the back of the house, but not to break the glass."

"She meant that clue for her father," Benny said. "I guess he would have known what it was about."

Mrs. Wren said, "I've never been in your house. But once Stephanie showed me a photograph of the house. She wanted to get a frame for it to surprise her father."

"That photograph is hanging in my room right now," Rory said.

"Think of that!" exclaimed Mrs. Wren. "After all these years!"

Benny said, "Rory has our guest room. That's the room Stephanie had. The furniture is different, but nobody changed the pictures."

"On the back of the house," Mrs. Wren said slowly. "You're sure she didn't write 'in the back of the house'?"

"No," Rory said, "it's very plain. And the back of the house has all been changed. That's what Henry said."

Benny looked around the Jenny Wren Shop. He wished there was something he could buy. But everything was for sewing or knitting.

Some buttons were on the counter. They were sewed on cards. One set of buttons caught Benny's eye. The buttons looked just like coins.

All at once something clicked in Benny's mind. He said, "Come on, Rory! I'll race you home on our bikes! Let's go."

"Why are you in such a hurry all of a sudden?" Rory asked.

"Wait and see," Benny said. "Good-bye, Mrs. Wren. Something here just gave me a new idea. If it helps, I'll let you know. Let's go, Rory."

It didn't take long for the boys to ride home.

"Have you thought of some place new to look?" Rory asked. "Do you think you know where the coins are?"

"We'll find out," Benny said, and he climbed up the stairs ahead of Rory. He ran into Rory's room.

"Here in my room?" Rory asked. "Where?"

Benny didn't say a thing. He walked over to the wall by Rory's bed. He took down the framed photograph of the house, the one made when Stephanie lived there.

"What are you going to do with that?" Rory asked. "We looked at that picture and took it down the first day I was here. I remember that."

"That's right," Benny said. "We looked at the picture. But remember what Stephanie said, 'Look on the back of the house.' " As he said this, Benny turned the picture over.

" 'Don't break the glass,' " Rory said. "Benny, do you think she meant the glass on the front of the picture?"

"I do!" said Benny. "Look—there's cardboard on the back. We looked before and saw these little nails that hold the cardboard in place. I'm going to take them out."

Rory held his breath while Benny tried to pull the small nails loose. But they were rusty and would not come out. His fingers weren't strong enough.

"I'll get the pliers," Rory said. "What do you expect to find? Another clue?"

Benny shook his head. "I have another idea. You get the pliers. I'll wait."

Benny shook the picture gently. Nothing rattled. But Benny did not look disappointed. He waited, and Rory ran into the room with the pliers.

Violet followed Rory. She said, "I heard you boys come in. What is it?"

"I have an idea," Benny said. "Perhaps I understand what Stephanie was telling her father."

He took the pliers. He pulled out the rusty nails as fast as he could. They came out easily.

"Lift out the cardboard, Ben," Rory said. "Be careful. It's very old."

Benny pried off the cardboard. It was not easy to get out. As he lifted it up he caught his breath. There was something under the cardboard.

Benny, Violet, and Rory saw what was behind the cardboard at the same time. "Oh, oh!" they exclaimed. "There they are!"

Nobody moved. They sat and gazed at the back of the photograph as if they were stunned.

The back of the photograph was covered with the same blue cloth as the coin case. The coins were stuck on the cloth in neat rows of five, glued in place.

As soon as they were over the first surprise, Rory said, "They are on the back of the house! And we didn't have to break the glass!"

"How did you ever think of looking there?" Violet asked.

Benny laughed and said, "You'll never guess. I got the idea in the Jenny Wren Shop."

"Tell me," Violet begged.

"Well, there were buttons like coins sewed on cards," Benny said. "We'd been thinking about the coins stacked in a little box or something. We never thought how easy it would be to spread them out—just like this."

Rory nodded. "They don't take up much room. Nobody ever guessed they were in the picture frame. How many are there?"

Benny counted. There were five rows and ten coins in each row. That made fifty coins altogether. Big ones, little ones, gold ones, and copper ones.

This was the old Blue Collection that Stephanie Shaw had made so many years ago!

Violet was the first to speak. She said, "Of course the first thing to do is to show them to Grandfather. I know he hoped we would find them."

Benny said, "Here, Violet, you carry the coins. They are sure to drop off if I try it."

Violet lifted the picture very slowly and the three children went down the stairs to Mr. Alden's home office.

As they were almost at the foot of the stairs, Benny called out, "Found! Found! We have found the coins, Grandfather!"

Henry and Jessie heard Benny. Henry called, "Ben! You found them? I can't believe it!"

"You don't mean the Blue Collection? The whole of it?" demanded Mr. Alden. He got up quickly from his desk.

"I think so," answered Benny. "They are all stuck on blue cloth."

"Bright blue," added Violet. "Like the cases."

Grandfather sat down again. Violet laid the coins on the desk in front of him.

"I can't believe it!" said Grandfather. "I just can't believe that these are the coins from little Stephanie Shaw."

Grandfather looked sharply at the coins. He tried to lift one to see the back. "Stuck with glue," he said. "Now where did you children find this?"

"Turn it over, Granda, and you'll see," said Rory. He was having the time of his life.

Mr. Alden turned the whole cardboard over and saw the photograph.

Henry exclaimed, "Right on the back of the very picture of our house. Stephanie told the truth. It is on the back of the house."

"And her father never found it," Violet said, a little sadly.

"I guess Stephanie thought the Shaws were coming back. Or perhaps something kept her father from following the clues," Jessie said. "So the coins have been safely hidden all this time."

Violet said suddenly, "We promised to tell Mrs. Wren if we found the coins. I'll telephone the shop."

She went at once to the telephone. Soon the family heard her say, "Yes, Mrs. Wren. We'll come over soon to tell you the whole story. You'll hardly believe it."

Then she came back and sat down with the others.

"What are we going to do with the coins?" Benny asked his grandfather.

"Well, I think the time has come to call my friend, Professor Nichols," he said.

"Will he come?" asked Benny.

"Oh, he'll come all right if he hears the word 'coin,'" said Mr. Alden. "You children will have to get another room ready for a guest."

"That's nothing," said Benny. "Getting a room ready is the best thing we do."

"When will you call him, Granda?" asked Rory. He wanted to see this professor who knew so much.

"This very minute," said Mr. Alden with a smile. "When he comes, you must all be ready for his strange looks. He is a rather odd person. His hair is snow white, although he is not any older than I am. He never wears a hat, not even in winter. He is a wonderful person. You will be lucky to meet him."

Mr. Alden found the telephone number and in a moment he was saying, "Hello, Andrew. This is James Alden."

"You don't say so!" answered a booming voice. The children could hear every word. "What's the trouble?"

"No trouble," replied Grandfather. "Just a few old coins turned up. My—"

"Say no more," interrupted Professor Nichols. "I'll come as soon as I can get a plane. You knew I'd say that, didn't you?"

Grandfather laughed and answered, "We'll meet your plane. You'll know me because I will have five young people with me."

"I'd know you anyway, anywhere," said the professor's voice. "Without any children at all."

As Mr. Alden hung up the telephone he said, "Same old friend! Same old Andrew!"

"It's lucky that you know Professor Nichols, Grandfather," Benny said. "I don't know anyone at all who could help us with the coins. But I guess we could have gone to the library for a book on coin collecting."

"Yes, I'm sure the library has many books on coins," said Grandfather with a quick nod. "But Professor Nichols is a real expert. He is just the man to ask about the hidden coins. After all, he knew Stephanie and her father many years ago."

A day later Henry drove the station wagon to the airport. The Aldens could hardly wait for the plane to come in. When they saw Professor Nichols leaving the plane, they knew that Mr. Alden was right.

People stared at the great man. His long white hair blew in the light breeze.

"I came right away, James," said Professor Nichols. "You know I will go almost anywhere if I can find a new coin."

Mr. Alden said, "I know that very well, Andrew. I'm glad to get some coins together just to get you to come here to visit me. We have about fifty coins."

"I can hardly wait to see them," said the professor.

Henry had already turned the car around and was driving out of the airport.

"And the coins? Shall I see them at once?" asked the visitor.

"Just as soon as we get home, Andrew," said Grandfather, smiling at Jessie. "I told you he would not pay much attention to anything but coins."

The minute the car stopped in the driveway in front of the Alden house, they all took the professor into the dining room. The blue card was on the table before him.

CHAPTER 10

What It All Meant

Professor Nichols sat down at the dining room table and began to look at the coins. From an inside pocket he took a magnifying glass like one Benny had seen a watchmaker use. He fitted it into his eye.

Rory and the Aldens leaned excitedly on the table, watching the professor.

"What a sight! What a sight," he murmured, almost to himself. "Oh, my, oh, my!"

Suddenly Professor Nichols put his finger on a gold coin.

"Look here!" he exclaimed, speaking to Benny who was nearest. "There are only ten coins like this in the whole wide world! You can see it is a four dollar gold piece. And here is one of the ten!"

"That makes the collection valuable, doesn't it?" Benny asked.

"Valuable? Valuable? Oh, yes. It is priceless! Now look. Here is a twenty-cent piece. Did any of you ever hear of a twenty-cent piece?"

"No," they all answered. They were fascinated by the professor and all he knew about the coins.

"Well, no wonder. These twenty-cent pieces didn't last long. You can see that they would get mixed up with quarters. That made a lot of trouble. Nobody liked the coins. Very soon they weren't made anymore. I haven't seen one of them for years, and I don't own one myself."

"How can you tell if it is a real twenty-cent piece?" asked Benny. "We don't know a thing about coins."

Professor Nichols took the magnifying glass from his eye and smiled at Benny. "Of course you don't. I'm glad to tell you. Look here. Feel the edge of this coin. It has a smooth edge for one thing. I'll take a quarter out of my pocket. You see, the edge is milled. That means it has little ridges."

"I see," Rory said. "The edge of the twenty-cent piece is smooth."

"That's right," the professor said. "Now look at the figure of the woman on the coin. She's the goddess Liberty and she is often on older U. S. coins. But here on the twenty-cent piece she is sitting down. A coin collector calls this 'Liberty Seated.' If there were only Liberty's head shown, it would be a different coin altogether."

"Are all these coins valuable?" asked Mr. Alden.

"Oh, yes. Even the pennies are valuable. Somebody knew what he was doing when he collected these.

However, the gold piece and the twenty-cent piece are the best of all."

"What about that Indian-head penny?" Jessie asked.

Professor Nichols smiled. "A lot of people like to collect pennies. Some pennies are very hard to find and that makes them worth a lot. But most of the pennies here are worn. That makes them of less value. They're interesting to people just beginning to collect coins."

Henry said, "All of these coins are forty years old at least."

The professor said, "This may surprise you. Sometimes the oldest coin is not worth the most. I have coins from Roman times that are not worth as much as some of these U. S. coins. That's because the fewer there are, the more each one is worth."

"I see," Benny said. "That's interesting."

Rory nodded. "Aye," he said softly.

Professor Nichols turned to Mr. Alden. "James," he said, "this is an unusual collection. And it is put together in an unusual way. There must be a story behind it. Who owns it?"

"I really don't know," said Grandfather. "But we know who used to own it. The children found the coins after a great hunt. They followed a lot of false clues. One clue said 'Look on the back of the house.' *You* look, Andrew, on the back of that coin card."

Professor Nichols carefully turned the cardboard over and saw the photograph.

"This very house!" he said. "I'm beginning to get some ideas."

Grandfather looked at Violet and asked, "You still have the coin case, don't you? Will you get it for the professor?"

Violet went to the hall stairs and ran up to her room.

The professor could not sit still. He pushed back his chair and walked back and forth, waiting for Violet. He did not wait long. She was soon back and put the blue case into his hand.

The professor could not speak for a minute. He

said, "Of course I know this! A little girl—Stephanie Shaw—made this. I knew her father. I helped her a little on this collection myself."

Mr. Alden said, "Then we are right. This is the Blue Collection."

"It certainly is. I never knew what became of it after the Shaws went to France. Has it been hidden here all this time? I can't understand why no one ever claimed it."

"The children learned that the Shaw family died in France many years ago," Mr. Alden said. "Benny found Stephanie's journal hidden behind a loose board in a closet wall."

"Rory helped, too," Benny said.

Rory added, "The empty coin case was there, Granda."

"We'll show you all the clues," Benny offered.

Professor Nichols said, "What a story! It is a wonderful collection that might easily have been lost forever. Oh, I don't like to think that I might have missed this collection entirely!" He shuddered. "I would indeed like to see all of the things you found."

"Here is Stephanie's journal," said Violet. "I brought that down, too."

"It is her writing," said Professor Nichols. "And you children worked out the mystery? I never could have done it."

"What do you think we should do with this collection?" asked Henry. "Should we keep it or sell it? Would anybody buy it?"

"*I* would!" said Professor Nichols. "There are valuable coins in this collection. It would give me great happiness to own it. However, I don't want to take the famous Blue Collection away from you children."

Benny said, "You knew Stephanie. I think you should have it."

"I'll tell you what I'll do," the professor said. "I'll pay you for the Blue Collection. Then I'll select some special coins for each one of you."

He quickly pulled five coins off the blue cloth from different places on the card. He gave one to each of the Aldens and Rory.

"There!" he said. "You Aldens can start your own collection. I think you'll enjoy it."

"Start a collection with four coins?" exclaimed Benny.

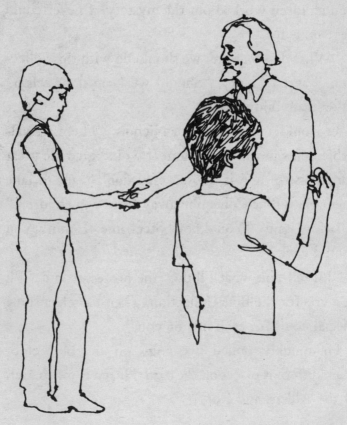

The professor nodded. "You'll be surprised how quickly you'll add more coins. The minute people know that you are making a collection, they will help you."

"I think I'll collect Canadian coins," Rory said. "I'm visiting the Aldens. I'm from Canada."

"You are?" said Professor Nichols with a sharp look at the boy. "Maybe you have a Canadian five-cent piece with a beaver on it. And there's a famous silver dollar from 1947 with men paddling a canoe. Some of the early fur traders, I guess. Yes, you can have an exciting collection."

That evening at dinner, Professor Nichols looked at Benny and Rory. He said, "You boys are hiding part of the mystery about the Blue Collection from me."

"We're not!" Benny exclaimed. "We showed the journal and the clues and told you about the Jenny Wren Shop. That's all there is."

The professor shook his head. "I'll tell what I'm wondering about. How did you boys happen to find the empty coin case and the papers in the closet wall?"

Benny said, "That's easy. Vacation came and I was lonesome."

"You were?" asked the professor and laughed. "I can't believe that! But I still don't understand."

"Well, you see," Benny explained, "all my friends were away and I was lonely. So Grandfather invited Rory to come."

"That's right," Rory said. "Mrs. McGregor knows my family. That's how it happened."

"Of course Rory had to have the room next to mine," Benny went on. "We didn't know anything about Stephanie then or that it had been her room."

Professor Nichols smiled. He could see that the only way to get the whole story was to let Benny tell it his way.

Benny went on, "We had rooms next to each other. That made us think of a telegraph between them. We thought we'd run a cord through holes in our closet walls."

"It was a good idea," Rory said. "But then we found all this stuff in the hole. Say, Benny, we never did finish our telegraph!"

"That's right," Benny exclaimed. "I guess our next mystery is how to make it work."

The other Aldens and Professor Nichols all laughed.

"If you can't find a mystery, make one," the professor said.

Benny added, "And I'll tell you something else, I'm not lonesome anymore."

"Good!" said Grandfather. "That's all I want."

GERTRUDE CHANDLER WARNER discovered when she was teaching that many readers who like an exciting story could find no books that were both easy and fun to read. She decided to try to meet this need, and her first book, *The Boxcar Children*, quickly proved she had succeeded.

Miss Warner drew on her own experiences to write the mystery. As a child she spent hours watching trains go by on the tracks opposite her family home. She often dreamed about what it would be like to set up housekeeping in a caboose or freight car—the situation the Alden children find themselves in.

When Miss Warner received requests for more adventures involving Henry, Jessie, Violet, and Benny Alden, she began additional stories. In each, she chose a special setting and introduced unusual or eccentric characters who liked the unpredictable.

While the mystery element is central to each of Miss Warner's books, she never thought of them as strictly juvenile mysteries. She liked to stress the Aldens' independence and resourcefulness and their solid New England devotion to using up and making do. The Aldens go about most of their adventures with as little adult supervision as possible—something else that delights young readers.

Miss Warner lived in Putnam, Connecticut, until her death in 1979. During her lifetime, she received hundreds of letters from girls and boys telling her how much they liked her books. And so she continued the Aldens' adventures, writing a total of nineteen books in the Boxcar Children series.